# *THE FIRE*

To Alfredo Rimoch…a true friend,
and of course to Carlo, Fabio and Alexis
F V B

Groundwood Books / Douglas & McIntyre
720 Bathurst Street, Suite 500, Toronto, Ontario M5S 2R4

Distributed in the USA by Publishers Group West
1700 Fourth Street, Berkeley, CA 94710


National Library of Canada Cataloguing in Publication Data
Janisch, Heinz
The fire : a folktale from Ethiopia
ISBN 0-88899-450-8
1. Friendship—Folklore.  I. VandenBroeck, Fabricio
II. Title.
PZ8.1.J36Fi 2002      j398.2'096307      C2002-900538-8

Library of Congress Control Number:  2002102248


The illustrations are in acrylics on paper prepared with a textured ground.
Printed and bound in China by Everbest Printing Co. Ltd.

# THE FIRE

An Ethiopian Folk Tale

*Retold by* Heinz Janisch

*Illustrated by* Fabricio VandenBroeck

## A GROUNDWOOD BOOK

Douglas & McIntyre

Toronto  Vancouver  Buffalo

IN A LAND not far from here lived a man who was a slave. Every day he worked in his master's cotton fields from sunrise until dark. When he came home he cleaned the master's house. After that it was time to feed the animals. Then he had to chop wood. He often worked until midnight.

Time passed, and the man who was a slave was so tired that he became ill.

One day he could no longer stand his life. He went to his master and said, "I have been your slave for such a long time. You have often promised me freedom. Tell me, what can I do to be free at last?

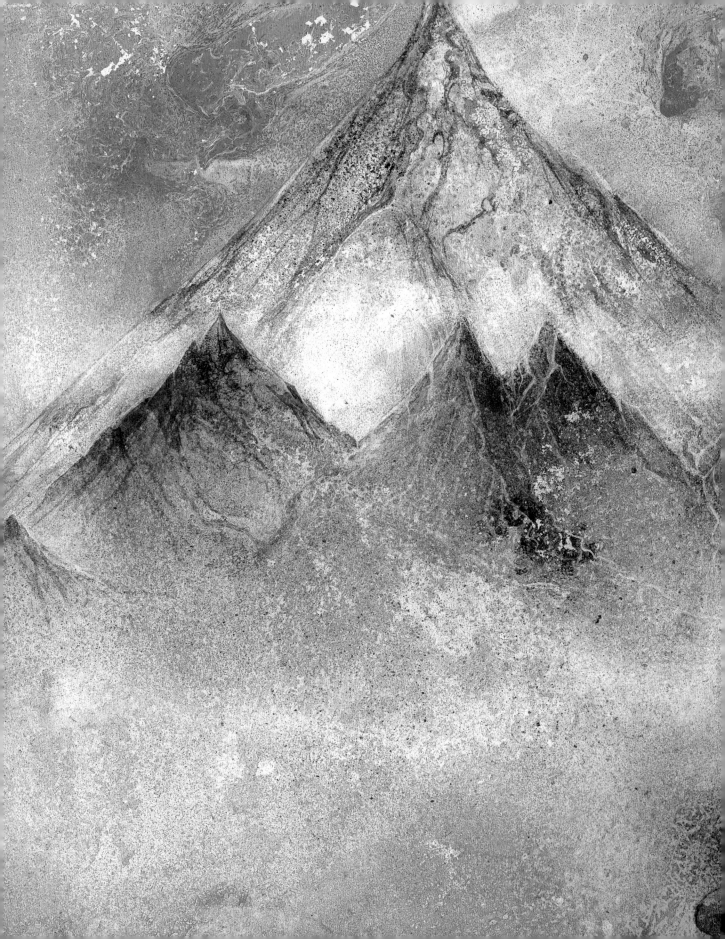

His master laughed at him. "You want to be free? I'll tell you what you can do! See that mountain over there? Go and climb that mountain tonight. It is covered with snow and ice. The air is so cold that your breath will freeze. You must stand there until day breaks.

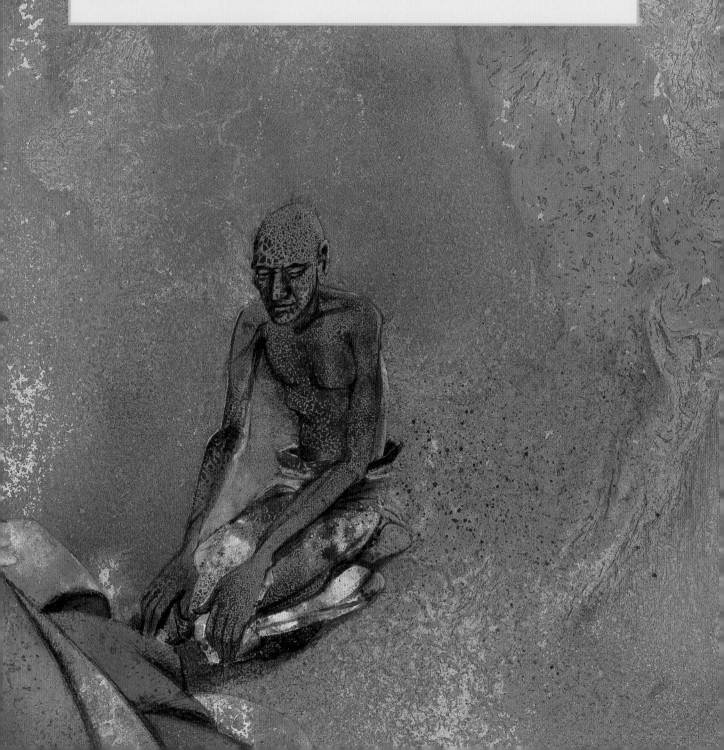

"If you can survive all night without clothes or shelter, as naked as the rocks around you, then I will free you. No one will lend you a hand. No one will cover you with a warm cloak. You will be naked and alone."

The man went to his best friend, who was a wise old man.

"What should I do?" he asked. "How will I survive this night? I will go up the mountain, and I will die from the cold."

His friend thought about it.
"I will help you," he said after a while.

At twilight, the man climbed to the top of the mountain on the edge of the village.

Meanwhile his friend, heavily laden with firewood, climbed to the top of the next mountain.

The man who was a slave stood barefoot in the snow that covered the mountain top. He had taken off his clothes. He shivered with cold. The rocks around him were covered with ice. He hardly dared to breathe.

Suddenly, on the next mountain, a fire blazed up, burning with bright high flames.

The man saw it in the distance, a light in the darkness.

Beside the fire he could just see his friend. He saw him struggling to keep the fire burning, feeding it with wood, making sure that it did not go out as the wind fanned the flames.

The man who was a slave gazed at this fire. He was naked and surrounded by snow and ice, but he was no longer freezing. The fire in the darkness, the fire that burned for him, kept him warm.

All night long he watched the fire and felt its warmth, and the cold did not harm him.

The next morning, when it grew light, he climbed down from the mountain and went to his master.

His master was angry. He did not want to set the slave free, but he had no choice.

"Go," he said.

The man who had survived the long cold
night was no longer a slave.
He was now a free man.
And so he went.